DIARY OF A ROBLOX NOOB JAILBREAK
BOOK 1

Legal Notice

Copyright (c) 2019 Rob Xena.

Diary of a Roblox Noob Jailbreak

Book 1

By: Rob Xena

Contents

Monday..8

Tuesday...18

Wednesday...29

Thursday..38

Friday..53

Monday

My name is Ethan. I've been stuck in this prison cell for a while now. I would say about a month or so.

But who knows, it could be much more. I tend to lose track of time in these spaces. Anyway, they got the wrong guy.

I really wasn't supposed to ever be here, because I never did anything wrong.

But no one seems to really care whether or not I deserve to be here. The important thing is – I have a plan to get out.

I remember the arrest like it was yesterday. Which again maybe it was because I'm not very good at telling time, but that's ok.

They just all appeared out of nowhere and took me to the car.

They were saying something about a robbery, but I've never done such a thing in my life!

And now look at me.

Stuck in a cell. It's not too bad of a cell, to be honest.

But the point is that I'm not supposed to be here.

There's a bed to sleep on, regular food and water, and it's warm. But the room is too small.

I'm one of those people who get really weird with the feeling on being a closed space.

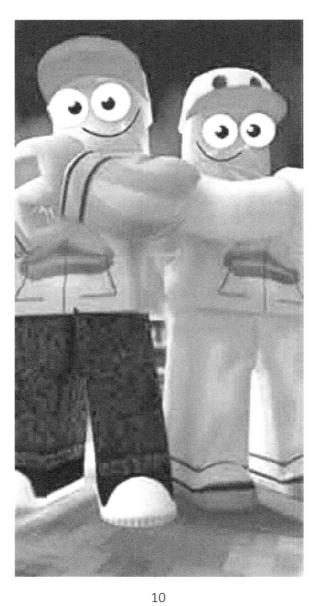

Not sure how many other people out there can relate, but it's tough, man. It takes a lot of focus for me to not be bored in such a small space. I can't even have a book with me to read!

I don't think that anyone else is having a better time than me to be honest. I can see the other people in the cells around them, and everyone seems bored out of their mind. Not sure how I should feel about this. They look like they are trying everything they can think of to just not be bored. I don't think it's working for them.

But who knows, maybe there are more people in here who also should not be here. I wonder if I will be able to meet anyone new who can help me with this escape. Who knows. Maybe someone else is just as excited as me to use this amazing escape opportunity that's coming up.

I only found out about it by accident. Only because I heard a few others talk about it yesterday when we were outside in the yard for exercise. They said that we will soon be moved to a maximum security prison. In about two weeks. That's a huge problem for me.

It's huge because I don't know if I would ever be able to actually escape from such a thing. this

prison that I'm in right now is bad enough. What will I do if they actually do take me to a maximum security prison? There is no way that I can get out of it!

Anyway, I didn't hear anyone else wanting to actually escape this prison, but I have a feeling that there may be a few ideas going around in their heads. A few really good ides on how we can get out of there. But I can't really rely on anyone.

Whenever you have a plan that's this big, it's important that you only include the people who are just as passionate as you about it. You need people who will follow all the rules and stick by you even when things get tough.

The problem is that I haven't been here for long enough to learn about this. I haven't met many of the others, and I only know a few names myself. This is because we are not really allowed to communicate with each other much in here.

I usually meet people either when we are eating, or when we are allowed to go outside. Some are friendly, but no one is too friendly. Hey, I don't blame them. You can never be too sure in these situations. You never know if someone in here might be a spy who is trying to figure what is going

on behind the scenes when the police are not looking.

That would actually be a good plan for them. To put an undercover police officer among us so that he can see what's really going on. Just the thought of it scares me! No, I should probably try to do this escape on my own just in case.

If I get caught in my escape plan then I will actually be guilty for sure and there will be no way for me to escape a penalty. That really doesn't sound like a good life to live at all. No, I have to be careful. If I can trust someone, then of course I would love to help them escape, too. Let's see what happens.

There is this one guy who is in the cell right in front of me. I've been watching him for a few days, both inside his cell and outside of it. He looks very shy and seems to stick to himself all the time. I am not sure that he is someone who would like to make a new friend or try something dangerous.

But you never know what is going on in someone's head. Maybe I could get to talk to him the next time that we are outside of here. Who knows, maybe we have the same things in common and the same wish to escape from here.

I think I can hear the guards coming for today's lunch shift. They always take us out of our cells for lunch under heavy security. I love the lunch but I don't love the security process. However, the lunch is actually a very important part of my escape plan. And maybe the guy in the other cell can help me.

Today, I will try to talk to him and to see if we can get something going together about the escape plan. I cannot imagine anyone wanting to stay here for however long, so let's see if we can help each other out.

Tuesday

Yesterday was a great day! I never even realized that it was going to be so good! I was convinced that I would never be able to meet someone who had the same dreams as me of escaping this place. But I was wrong!

The guys that I mentioned from the cell opposite mine, his name is Johnny. And yes, he really is super shy. He is just as shy as I thought that he was going to be. In fact, maybe even more than I thought he was going to be.

However, once I started talking to him he almost became a completely different person. I was so impressed. He doesn't say much, but the things that he does say are very honest and he even seems kind. It isn't easy to be kind when you have been arrested, but he is.

He was sitting on his own at one of the tables. I thought about it for a long time. Whether or not I should say hi and see if he would talk to me. Finally, I got the courage to speak to him.

"Hello," I said.

He looked super weird about being spoken to. I was almost certain that he would not respond and just go back to his food. But he did respond.

"Hello," said Johnny.

"I am in the cell opposite you," I said.

"I know," he replied.

He then just went back to eating his food. I decided to be a little closer to him so that I could have a better conversation. I was also worried that maybe some of the others that were watching us would make the whole thing a lot more difficult.

"How's it going?" I asked.

"About as well as it can possibly go in a prison," said Johnny.

"Did you know that they are planning on moving us?" I asked.

I am not sure if I should have waited a little longer before telling him this. But the problem with lunch is that it does not last long. So I had to really make sure that I was making the most of this one opportunity that I had to become friends with him.

"What do you think about that?" I asked him.

"What is there to think about?" he responded. "There is really nothing that I can actually do about it, is there?"

"I supposed not," I said. "But I was just thinking... imagine what the security will be like in the highest security prison? I mean, we will just be stuck there forever, right?"

He thought about this for a moment. I realized that he was a very smart guy. He was definitely putting everything together. At one point, I was absolutely certain that he knew exactly what I was talking

about. But would he want to be part of it?

"What are you suggesting?" he asked.

"I don't know yet," I said.

I tried to make it seem as if I wasn't really planning anything special. Not because I didn't want Johnny to be part of it, but because I honestly didn't want anyone else to know about it. What if they went straight to the police and told them about my plan?

"I was thinking..." I continued, "I have this plan that might help us out along the way."

"Are you suggesting we try to break out of a prison?" he said.

"Pretty much," I replied.

He looked at me like this was the last thing that he had in mind. But I also think that he was hoping that I would say something like that.

"How are we going to do it?" he asked.

"Well, it won't be easy," I said. "But I have been working on this plan for quite some time now and something tells me that it's going to work."

"How can you be so sure?" he asked.

"I can't. But I am hoping for the best, because this is the only chance that we will ever get. Also I need you to promise that you won't share this information with anyone," I said.

"Of course not. We would be in a lot more trouble than we are in now if anyone ever found out," he replied.

"Exactly," I said, "I am so glad that you understand the situation the way I do."

"Where do we start?" he asked.

"I'll let you know when the time is right. For now, just behave like you normally would and wait for my signal. My cell is across from yours, I will make sure to let you know when the time is right," I said.

He seemed quite please with this plan. He looked a lot braver than I had ever seen him. I was very excited about everything and I was already hoping that everything would eventually turn out alright.

I was delighted to have found a new friend and companion in this mission of mine. But in order for the mission to succeed completely, I knew that I

would really have to do everything in my power to make sure that the plan was so perfect that nothing could ever go wrong. But is such a plan ever possible?

After the lunch, I went back to my room and lied on the bed. I spent a long time staring at the ceiling, but what I was actually doing was thinking about the plan over and over again. I had to make sure that I understood every single detail of the plan, otherwise it would fail.

The thing that was so scary for me was the fact that we only had one chance to be successful and that's it! Imagine if we did something wrong and things didn't go according to plan? How would we ever get our lives back to a normal place?

I was determined this time. I had never tried something like this before, but now that I had a new friend that wanted to help me, I knew that I had a much better chance of succeeding than ever before!

Wednesday

The excitement about my plan of escape was still there, but now I was definitely more afraid than

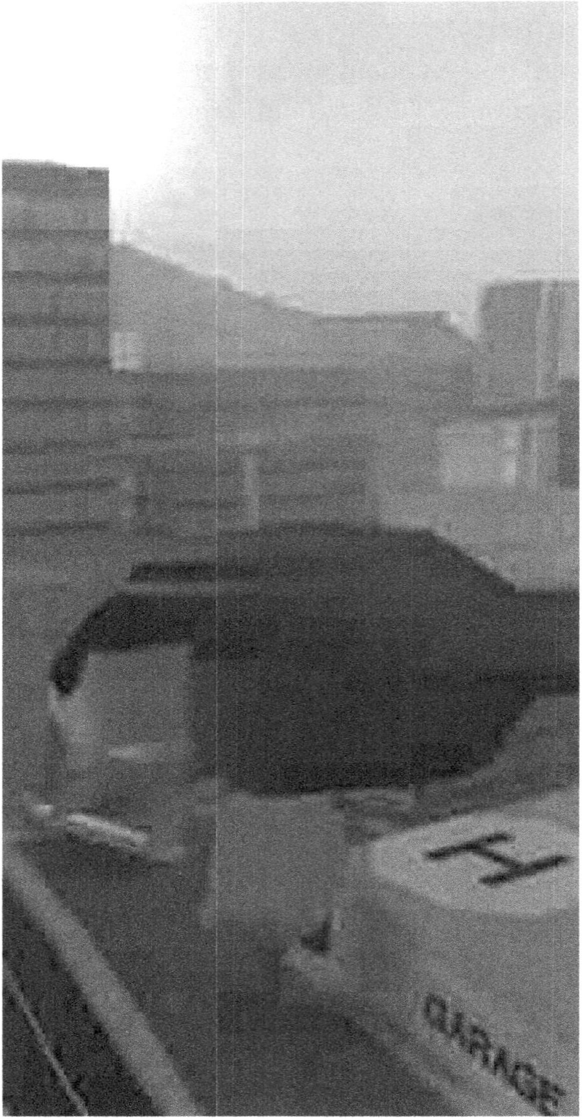
GARAGE

before. What if I did something wrong and Johnny had to pay the price. No. I would really have to make sure that everything was going to go perfectly well, otherwise there was really no point in doing this at all.

My plan was to break into the police room where they change their clothes. It's a special room where all the police uniforms are kept. My plan is to break into there and to steal two uniforms. One for me and one for Johnny.

Then, we would need to hide these stolen uniforms somewhere safe, and when the time is right, to change into them. This is definitely going to be the most difficult part. Although this prison may not be as strongly guarded as the others, there were still guards everywhere.

The only time that we would be able to do both of these things was either during a lunch break or during an exercise break. I thought about both options a lot. Being outside in the exercise means that there are many of and not that many guards. But it is very difficult to separate yourself from so many others.

The other option, the one for lunch, seemed like a

little bit of a better option. This is because we had the opportunity to use bathroom breaks for lunch. We couldn't use them often, but sometimes, if you are not feeling well, a kind guard will let you use the restroom.

This would be our only chance to steal the clothes because the guard changing room was close by. But in order to achieve this, both Johnny and I would have to go to the toilet at the same time. Who would let two of us leave at the same time?

Also, I really didn't know how good Johnny would be at something like this. He always looked so nervous. What if he made a mistake the guards saw that he was up to something? Well, now that I have already recruited him for the job, there would really be no other way than to continue with that we have already started to do.

I stood up from my bed and looked at Johnny's cell. He was also bored on his own. Every now and then he would look at me to wait for instructions. When I saw him looking at me, I made a few motions with my hands to tell him that our plan will start tomorrow.

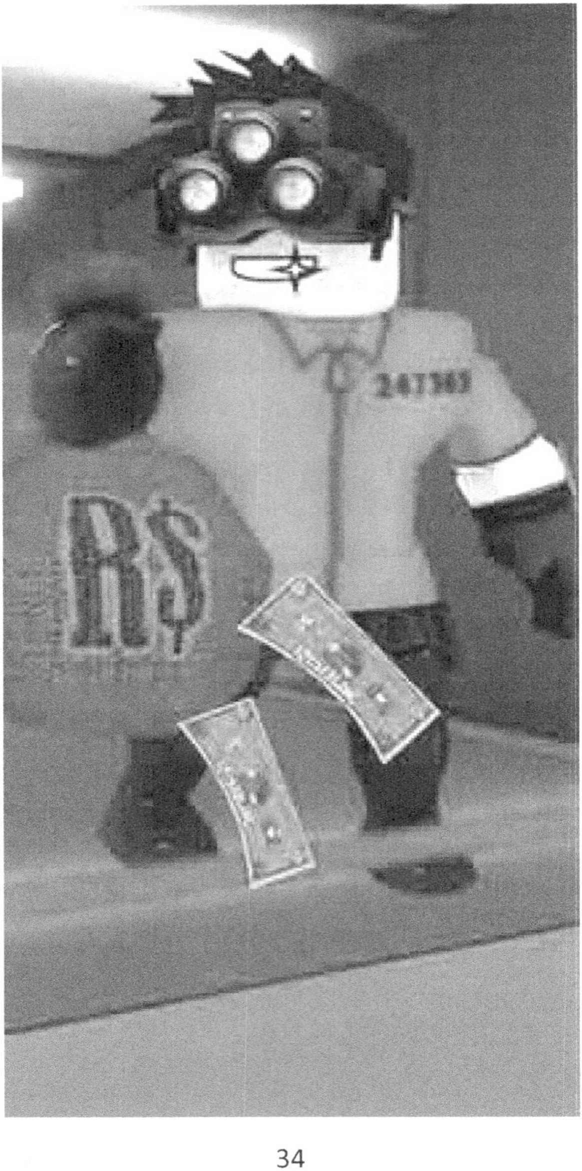
R$

He just nodded his head and he seemed to be pleased that we would be starting with this plan very soon. I am happy to have someone to help me with this. Although at first I wanted to do this on my own, everything is more difficult when you have to do it on your own.

For example, I am very good at breaking through doors, but in order to do this properly, I need someone to watch my back. Someone needs to be able to tell if someone else is coming. It is very important that we remain safe at all times. Like I said, if we make one mistake that's it.

There was not much that I could tell Johnny while I was still in my cell, so I knew that the only way that I would be able to do this properly is to wait until lunch tomorrow and to then try to secretly explain the clothes-stealing plan. I wonder if he will like it.

I gave him a quick nod that we understood each other, and then I went back to lie on my bed. I tried very hard to fall asleep, but it was so difficult to do this. But there was something inside me that made me sure that we were going to make it.

I did not commit the crime that I am here for. I

don't deserve to be here. I should be outside living my life. This was my chance to do just this.

Thursday

Today was the day. It was the one chance that we had to really start this process of escaping. I was worried, yes. Because there was no room for error. But I was also very excited to finally get the opportunity to get out of here!

I waited patiently for lunchtime to come. Before the guard arrived, I went through the whole plan again. In my head, I also revised through all the way that a door can be broken into. I had seen the door before and it didn't seem that different from any of the others.

The most important thing in this situation is to remain calm and collected, and to really trust yourself that you can do this. Trusting in yourself is one of the first ways that you can actually move forward to achieving a goal. And I was certainly confident that I could do it.

After a while, I could hear a guard arriving to take

us away for lunch. Johnny seemed a little uneasy when he saw the guard in front of his cell, but I could definitely understand how he was feeling.

After a while, we found ourselves sitting in our usual dining hall, having lunch. Johnny and I were sitting at the same table because I really needed to talk to him. He knew nothing about the actual plan, only that it was happening today.

We ate our lunch properly, as if nothing unusual was about to happen. This was very important for the actual plan, and was the most important key for making sure that no one sees anything strange happening between us.

I slowly told the plan to Johnny, when I felt that there weren't many people looking at us or listening to our conversation.

"The key is that we both have to end up in the toilet around the same time," I said.

"What do you mean?" said Johnny.

"We have to get into their changing room which is near the toilet. We are going to steal two guard

uniforms," I said.

Johnny looked a little worried about this. Perhaps he was not expecting us to actually steal something from a guard. But then again, how else would we ever get the chance to accomplish our mission and get out of here?

I could tell that he was not giving up on our plan, he just wasn't expecting it to happen this way. But he was also determined. Something told me that, perhaps, he was not meant to be locked up in here either.

"We cannot go to the toilet at the same time," I said. "But I can see that there are more guards here today than usual. I think it is because there are some new guards here who are training for their positions. They probably know a lot less than the senior guards so when you choose one to ask to go to the toilet, only ask the new guards," I said.

I said this because I knew that the new guards would probably be a little scared of the criminals that were in here, and also because they would not be so careful about letting people leave at the same time.

"Ok," said Johnny. "Who goes first?"

I thought about it for a moment. Johnny was the new guys between the two of us, so it would probably be safer if he went first. I felt that I would have an easier time convincing the second guard to let me go to the toilet as well.

"You go first," I said. "I will go as soon as I can find a guard to let me too."

"Ok," said Johnny.

He continued to eat his lunch like we were not discussing anything serious. Soon, he saw that one of the younger, new guards was passing by us. He raised his hand up high.

"Excuse me," said Johnny.

The new guard approached him to see what he wanted.

"May I please go to the toilet?" asked Johnny.

The new guard looked around him for a little bit and then gave a slight nod with his head. Johnny was obviously free to leave. The new guard went to the other side of the room to check something with his boss.

I didn't even look up from my lunch when this was happening. I didn't want it to seem like I was doing anything suspicious either. I just kept my head down and let the situation pass as it needed to.

Johnny got up and left. I waited for about 10 minutes, and then I started to look around to find a guard of my own. There were so many new ones that it was actually difficult to pick one to ask. But soon, I found the perfect guard.

I did the same thing that Johnny did, which is to raise my hand to get the guard's attention. Soon, the guard also came to my table. This was a different guard so he didn't know that another person had already gone to the toilet.

"Excuse me," I said. "Can I please go to the toilet?"

"Sure, but come back quickly," said the guard.

He was obviously trying to sound dangerous and to scare me. Lucky for me, I didn't need a lot of time to complete the mission that I had set for myself and for Johnny. I quickly got up from my seat and headed straight for the toilets.

For a moment, I was worried that maybe Johnny

had become scared and ran off. This was a very serious thing that we were doing after all. Luckily, this was not the case.

When I entered the toilet, Johnny was pretending to wash his hands.

"How do we do this?" he asked.

"We need to get to the door of the changing room from here," I said. "This will not be too difficult because it is very close. Our biggest problem is that we don't have a lot of time before they figure out that we have been for too long."

"What do you need me to do?" asked Johnny?

"I just need you to watch my back and to make sure that I am not being watched by any weird guards. Trust, the last thing that we want is for them to see what we are doing," I said.

"Ok. Got it," said Johnny. "Let's go.

Slowly, we got out of the toilet and checked out if the cost was clear. It sort of was. It can never be empty in prison, but there were definitely not as many people as I was expecting them to be.

Everyone was so busy with the new guards and

their training that this really was the perfect moment to reach the changing room. We quickly moved over to the door.

Johnny did a great job keeping the situation clear. He really focused on everything that was happening around us, to make sure that we were not being watched or followed by any of the guards and even any of the other criminals.

I quickly started the process to break open the door. I fiddled with the lock here and there. It was a very simple lock, they were really not working hard to protect this section at all. It took me some time to open the door, but not long at all.

We entered the room right away and picked the first two uniform pairs that we saw. There was really no time to think about size. They all looked the same which is good, because it will help us to blend in more easily.

We quickly grabbed the uniforms and then went back to the toilet to hide them. this was the only place where we could safely leave the uniforms until tomorrow. After all, there is no other place where they could be hidden. Certainly not under out clothes or in our cells.

Once we were done, Johnny and I returned to the dining room and when back to eat our lunch. No one had suspected us of doing anything bad so they just left us to finish our lunch. We couldn't believe that we were able to get away with it!

After lunch, they took us back into our individuals cells. I went back to bed and started to plan the day tomorrow. There were many things that we would need to do correctly, but I was so confident that we would succeed.

Friday

I was very excited as soon as I woke up. This was the day that I would finally be able to escape the prison! It had been a long time now since I first arrived here. I was tired, and I really hated the place. And did I mention that I was not supposed to be here in the first place?

I did my best to act like nothing was happening for the entire morning. We would once again need to wait until lunchtime in order to get our chance to go to the toilet and change clothes. Lunchtime was a long way away and many things could change

54

until then to stop us from achieving our goal.

When the time arrived, as always, a guard came to pick up each one of us. The guard took us to our usual spots in the big dining room. We started to eat our lunch like nothing was happening. I was especially cautious to see if the new guards were still there.

Luckily, they were. I really needed these new guards to make sure that we could use the new clothes that we had stolen to blend in with them. Honestly, it was now or never. If we missed this chance, who knows when we would get a new chance again to try the same thing.

We followed the same plan as yesterday. Each of us found one of the new guards to let us use the toilet, separately. Once again, we managed to accomplish this mission. Although, once again, I was the one that got a grumpy new guard.

When Johnny and I were in the toilet, we quickly took out the clothes that we had stolen yesterday and immediately put them on. We checked ourselves out in the toilet mirror. We even had hats to put on as guards, which is great for keeping us camouflaged.

Now we had to figure out how we were going to leave the toilets without being noticed. The thing is, these toilets were not the ones that guards would use. But we had no other choice but to walk out.

Johnny peaked through the door a little bit to check if the coast was clear, and then we just quickly walked out of the toilet. Our plan was to go straight to the new guards that were being trained for their new posts.

We carefully blended in with a small crowd of them. they didn't notice that we were prisoners because they were also new here and they were not aware of who is who. The only way that they could tell the difference was through the clothes that were being worn.

Johnny and I also agreed that we would spend a little bit of time with the new guards before we left to go outside. We didn't want to spend any time talking to the guards, just to blend in a little and then to walk out.

After we were sure that we had spent enough time with the new guards, we slowly made our way to the exit that the guards use when they go home.

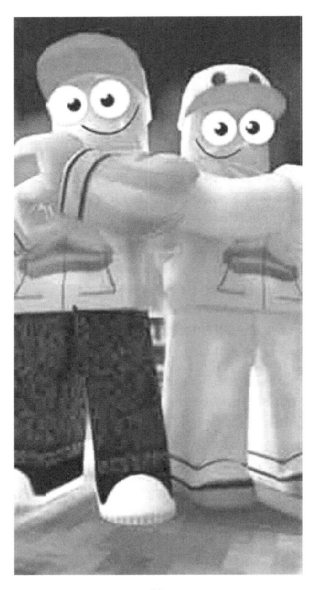

We were so scared that someone was going to find out that we were running away.

At that moment, a huge fight broke out on the other side of the dining room. All the other guards ran over there to break up the fight and to see what it going on. This was our biggest chance ever!

We quickly went straight for the door, gave a quick wave to the security guard who was working there, and then just walked out! As soon as we got outside, we quickened out pace and tried to get as far away from the prison as possible. We couldn't believe it!

"We did it!" shouted Johnny.

"I know!" I said. "But don't get too relaxed yet. There are still many things that could go wrong. Besides, they will eventually know that we have disappeared."

"Just keep walking", said Johnny.

And we did. We walked for a very long way until we though that we were clear enough of the prison. We were so amazed to be outside after such a long time. In fact, I then realized that I knew nothing more about Johnny other than the fact

that he really wanted to help me and to escape as well.

Who was Johnny? Why was he here? What did he want to do now that we were out? How was he going to live this life?

I was very curious to find out the answers to these questions. But first, we wanted to get some proper food to eat. We found a nearby diner and went straight inside. We were not yet worried that our faces would be all over the news, so this was the perfect chance to eat.

We had sandwiches and dessert and we talked a little bit about what had just happened. But not a lot because there were so many others in the diner too. It was a very good day.

Next, we had to figure out where we would go and how we would live our lives now that we were out. This would not be easy, because it means that we have to run from the guards for a long time. But who knows what could happen?

Made in the USA
Las Vegas, NV
23 July 2021